WIND RIDERS

SHIPWRECK IN SEAL BAY

RIDERS

SHIPWRECK IN SEAL BAY

WRITTEN BY **JEN MARLIN**

ILLUSTRATED BY **MARTA KISSI**

HARPER

An Imprint of HarperCollinsPublishers

Library of Congress Cataloging-in-Publication Data

Names: Marlin, Jen, author. | Kissi, Marta, illustrator.
Title: Shipwreck in Seal Bay / Jen Marlin ; illustrated by Marta Kissi.
Description: First edition. | New York, NY : Harper, [2022] | Series: Wind
    Riders ; #3 | Audience: Ages 6–10. | Audience: Grades 1–5. | Summary:
    "Max and Sofia must save harbor seals from an oil spill caused by a
    leaking boat engine in Scotland"— Provided by publisher.
Identifiers: LCCN 2021042647 | ISBN 9780063029354 (hardcover) | ISBN
    9780063029347 (paperback)
Subjects: CYAC: Sailboats—Fiction. | Magic—Fiction. | Harbor
    seal—Fiction. | Seals (Animals)—Fiction. | Oil spills—Fiction. |
    Wildlife rescue—Fiction. | LCGFT: Novels.
Classification: LCC PZ7.1.M372445 Sh 2022 | DDC [Fic]—dc23
LC record available at https://lccn.loc.gov/2021042647

Typography by Joe Merkel

22 23 24 25 26   PC/LSCC   10 9 8 7 6 5 4 3 2 1
❖
First Edition

For young readers who love animals and the earth.
Together, you can change the world.

With special thanks to Erin Falligant

CONTENTS

CHAPTER 1

THE KiTE iN THE WiND

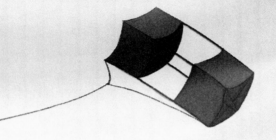

The wind tugged at the cherry-red box kite in Sofia's hands. It almost flew out of her grip. "Whoops!" she exclaimed. "Max, are you ready? It wants to fly!"

Max was hurriedly winding up the kite string. "Almost!" he called back.

He finished winding, then unraveled a little bit of line from the spool. "Okay," he said. "One, two . . . three!"

As Sofia let go, the kite strained at the line and floated straight up above them.

"It's working!" Sofia cried.

Max grinned. He lived with his grandpa, who was a retired fisher here in Starry Bay, and they had planned to go out in the boat this morning. But the wind was coming from the east, and Grandpa had told Max there was no point fishing when an easterly wind was blowing:

Wind from the west, fish bite the best.

Wind from the east, fish bite the least.

Wind from the north, do not go forth.

Wind from the south blows bait in their mouth.

It was an old proverb, and Grandpa believed in it.

But the east wind was perfect for flying kites!

The kite swooped low as the wind stopped gusting for a moment.

Max jogged across the sand, trying

to keep tension in the string, and almost tripped over a towel and a plastic shovel. He passed a trio of kids licking ice cream, then ran around a propped-up umbrella and toward the marina, where tourists watched from wrought-iron tables.

"Wait for me!" Sofia tightened her shoelaces and then raced after him. She was a strong runner, and she caught up with him on the boardwalk, near the edge of the mangrove forest.

As Max leaned over to catch his breath, the kite rippled in the wind.

The sight of it reminded Sofia of something.

"A scarlet macaw!" she said. "Doesn't it look like one?"

Max shot her another smile as he handed her the spool. He had known Sofia for only a short while, since her family had come to Starry Bay for the summer. But already, they shared a secret. They had discovered *Wind Rider*, a magical old boat that sailed to faraway places—like the Amazon rain forest, where scarlet macaws flew free.

Just a few yards away, within the mangrove forest, that magical old sailboat waited for them.

"Fly free, little kite," Sofia cheered as she held the string, but then she gasped as the kite dove toward the boardwalk, bounced twice, and landed on the dirt trail that led into the forest.

"Max, look!" She pointed. There, beside the downed kite, stood a bird. It shook sand from its gray feathers and cocked its smooth white head. Then it fixed its wise, dark eyes on Max.

"It's our seagull!" Max whispered. This was the mysterious bird that arrived whenever it was time for another adventure on *Wind Rider*.

"Are you sure?" asked Sofia.

"Yes!" Max started chuckling. "It's got a splotch of ice cream on its beak! It's an even messier eater than I am."

Sofia laughed, too. Their seagull friend was a notorious ice cream thief! They'd first met the bird when it had stolen hers.

As if in response, the gull bobbed its head. Then it flapped its wings and led them toward the mangrove forest.

"Let's go!" cried Sofia, racing ahead.

Max scooped up the kite and glanced back at the beach. How long would they be gone? He couldn't say for sure. But it didn't matter—no time would pass here in Starry Bay while they were away. No one would miss them. That was part of *Wind Rider*'s magic!

So he hurried after Sofia through the tangled hedge of roots and vines, puffing and panting to keep up with her.

The smell of seawater gave way to the smell of damp earth. Tree limbs crisscrossed overhead, dappling the path below with shadows.

The sailboat was so weathered and rotted that it seemed to melt into the ground. It rested sideways like a beached whale, half on land and half in the water. Max could just make out the words *Wind Rider* painted in white on the faded navy hull. Nobody who looked at it would have any idea that it was a magical boat.

Sofia had already climbed on deck.

She darted around the old mast and torn, musty sail. Then she lifted the heavy hatch that led to the cabin below. After scurrying down the rusty metal ladder, she hurried through the narrow cabin until she reached a wooden shelf.

"They're still here!" Sofia blew out a breath of relief. One half of a leathery turtle eggshell rested beside two red-and-blue macaw feathers, souvenirs of the

endangered animals she and Max had helped on their past adventures. *Where will the boat take us next?* she wondered. *Who needs our help this time?*

Up on deck, Max shivered. A brisk breeze had begun to blow, sending leaves swirling off branches. He heard the flutter of wings as the seagull swooped over his shoulder and landed on the deck beside him.

It's nearly time, Max realized. *We're about to set sail!*

He cupped his hands to his mouth. "Sofia!" he called.

Her smiling face appeared just as the wind began to pick up. She sprinted across the deck and crouched beside Max. They both touched the helm, which they knew set the magic in motion.

As the wooden helm began to spin, faster and faster, Max squeezed his eyes shut. He had one hand on the rail, and the other gripped the kite. The kite tugged, threatening to break free. . . . But just when he was sure he couldn't hang on any longer, the wind died down.

Sofia sprang up and let go of the

now-gleaming wooden rail. She felt a shiver of excitement as she saw crisp white sails overhead and a freshly polished deck beneath her feet. The *Wind Rider* looked brand-new! And it was sailing—fast— across a wide gray sea.

"Where are we now?" Max asked, opening his eyes. To his relief, he found that he was still holding on to the kite.

Together they stared at the rocky coastline ahead. Beyond the jagged cliffs, they saw rolling green hills and purple mountains that disappeared into misty clouds. By the shore was a village, a cluster of stone buildings and red-roofed houses. It was chilly here. Max tied the kite to the rail and wrapped his arms around himself.

Then Sofia spotted a flag flying from the cliffs above the harbor. She squinted until she could make it out. It was royal blue with a large white X across it. "Oh, I think I know!"

"Where?" asked Max, his heart racing.

"Scotland!" Sofia smiled widely. "I recognize the flag. My grandparents vacationed here—they told me it was a beautiful place with incredible wildlife. I've always wanted to come."

Goose bumps of excitement sprang up along Max's arms. He rubbed them down and grinned. He watched a bird dive and gracefully skim over the water. In the distance, something caught Max's eye—dark shapes moving across a cluster of rocks out in the sea.

Sofia saw them, too. "What are they?"

The deck shifted beneath her feet. *Wind Rider* slowly turned, arcing across the water as if to bring them closer to the animals.

Now Sofia could see their sleek heads and flippered bodies. She smiled. "I think they're seals!"

Chapter 2
SEALS IN A STORM

Max felt a gentle thud as *Wind Rider* dropped anchor near the rocks. The flippered sea animals turned their curious, puppylike faces toward the boat and greeted it with a chorus of grunts and barks.

Max studied their faces and spotted fur. "They *are* seals! And do you see their short muzzles? I think they're harbor seals!" he said.

"Really?" said Sofia. "I was hoping to see harbor seals in Starry Bay this summer!"

Max grinned. "I guess they have them in Scotland, too."

Six spotted seals rested on the rocks, watching the kids with their shiny black eyes. One sniffed the air while another settled lazily back down, rolling sideways as if to say, *No worries. They look friendly.*

Max pointed at a seal that lay on its belly, lifting its head and tail off the ground. "That one is shaped like a banana," he said, chuckling. The seal barked, as if in response.

A gust of wind swept across the sea, and the kite bobbed upward—along with every seal head.

"They like the kite!" Max said. He untied the string from the rail and let out more line, and the kite fluttered higher above the seals. They stared at it, scooching forward to get a closer look. "Maybe they think it's a bird."

Sofia laughed. "Maybe. Oh look, there's a baby!" She pointed as a seal—shorter and slightly less round than the others—nosed its way past its mother. Keeping its eyes on the kite, the pup lunged forward—and tumbled off the rock. Seconds later, its sleek head popped out of the waves. It splashed in a playful circle before its mother barked, calling it back out of the water.

Sofia's heart leaped. "It's so cute. I could watch it for hours!"

"Me too," said Max, but he shivered as he spoke. "At least until I turn into a

Popsicle. It's cold here. Should we look for jackets belowdecks?"

Sofia hesitated, but when the seals slid into the water—one by one—she sighed. "Yes, let's go see. Maybe we'll find clues down there about why *Wind Rider* brought us here!"

Max strode toward the hatch, winding up the line of his kite as he walked.

Like the deck above, the cabin of the sailboat looked shiny and new. The wooden shelf that held the turtle eggshell and macaw feathers gleamed in the light that poured through the portholes. Near the shelf, Sofia spotted a thick atlas resting on a table. The book flipped open and the pages flew, settling on a page showing a green mass of land surrounded on both sides and above by blue sea.

"Aha!" said Sofia, slapping the page. "We *are* in Scotland."

Behind her, Max yelped. When Sofia turned, she saw him standing beside a huge wooden chest. It was decorated with carvings of animals and always seemed to hold just what they needed for each adventure.

Max was tugging a woolen sweater over his head, but he appeared to be stuck. "Can I *mumble, mumble, mumble*?"

"Huh?" Sofia laughed as she pulled down gently on Max's sweater. Finally, his freckled face popped out the top.

"I said, can I get a little help here?" said Max. "Whew! This sweater is snug, but it sure is warm." The sea-blue sweater felt sturdy, yet light and soft. "There's one for you, too." Max tossed Sofia a reddish-orange sweater. She pulled hers on.

"So I guess *Wind Rider* knew we'd be cold," she said.

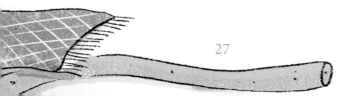

"Yes, and I have a feeling we'll be getting wet," Max announced. He pulled two life jackets out of the trunk, along with rain jackets. "Very wet."

Sofia laughed out loud. "It looks like it!"

"But what's with this big orange backpack?" asked Max. He lugged it out of the trunk, and it seemed stuffed full.

As he started to unzip it, Sofia stopped him.

"It's not a backpack," she said. She pointed to the words printed on the front.

"'Inflatable kayak,'" Max read. "Really? Cool!"

"Look, paddles!" Sofia announced, pulling them from the trunk. "And wet suits, too."

Max dug deeper and found some cozy cushions and extra-thick blankets. "Ooh, pool noodles! Are we going to be giving swimming lessons to someone?" He pulled out a long foam noodle and swung it playfully at Sofia.

She dodged, laughing.

As she turned, she spotted two steaming

mugs resting on the long wooden table in the galley. She hurried toward the table. "Hey—*Wind Rider*'s given us hot chocolate to warm up!" she exclaimed.

"Awesome!" The howling wind had crept through the deck hatch and cast a chill in the air, so hot chocolate sounded good to Max. He grabbed a blanket from the trunk and sat down next to Sofia, tucking the blanket over their laps. But as he took his first sip of hot chocolate, *Wind Rider* suddenly rocked sideways. "Whoa!" he cried. "I think it spilled."

Sofia glanced at the chocolaty mess. "Lucky for us, this thick blanket is soaking it right up."

As rain drummed hard on the deck and the boat started to heave up and down,

Sofia glanced through the portholes. "It's a storm." She chewed her lip, then jumped up and grabbed a rain jacket. "I'm going to check on the baby seal. What if it's separated from its mama?"

"The seals will be . . ." By the time Max uttered the word "fine," Sofia was gone. So he spread out the wet blanket to dry, grabbed his own rain jacket, and hurried after her.

As he poked his head through the hatch, the wind roared in his ears and rain whipped against his face, stinging his cheeks. Dark, threatening clouds hung overhead. How had the storm blown in so quickly? He carefully crossed the slippery deck toward Sofia.

Sofia gripped the rail with one hand and held her hood with the other. "I can't see the seals!" she cried.

Max searched the waves. "I can't, either," he said, raising his voice above the wind. "But they should be all right underwater." He wished he felt as confident as he sounded.

Then, from the corner of his eye, Max

spotted a patch of yellow. Something was being tossed side to side in the white-capped waves.

Uh-oh, that looks like a boat . . . and it's in trouble!

CHAPTER 3
LiTTLE BOAT LOST

Max gripped the wooden helm, trying to turn the wheel and force *Wind Rider* back toward the yellow boat. But the helm had a mind of its own. It slid beneath Max's fingers, turning in the *other* direction.

"Help me, it won't turn!" he called to Sofia. He could barely see her through the sheets of rain.

In seconds, she was beside him, tugging at the helm, too. "Why is *Wind Rider* taking us away from the boat?" she cried, her words quickly swallowed up in the storm.

"I don't know," said Max. He gritted his teeth. "But it's no use." He let go of the helm and let it spin. As he stood helplessly watching the yellow boat grow smaller and smaller, his stomach twisted. Would the people on board be okay?

"Maybe *Wind Rider* is taking us to get help," Sofia said hopefully.

She carefully walked along the slippery deck toward the bow. The sailboat was on course for the village they had seen. The blue flag whipped wildly from the cliffs above the harbor, which *Wind Rider* was quickly approaching.

As the boat slid alongside the dock, an older girl with wavy brown hair rushed out the front door of a red-roofed shop. She hurried onto the pier, all the way down it, then cupped her hand to her mouth. "Need help tying up?" she called in a thick accent.

"Thanks!" said Max. Rain lashed at his face as he threw a rope to her. Sofia and the girl worked to secure the rocking sailboat to the dock. Max lowered *Wind Rider*'s sails, then carefully stepped onto the wet pier to join them.

The girl beckoned them to follow her to

a nearby small open hut at the end of the dock. When they reached her, she held out her hand. "Hi, my name is Maisie."

"Hi." Max shook her hand. "I'm Max, and this is Sofia."

As Sofia shook Maisie's hand, she could see that the girl was only a year or two older than them.

"The water's too rough to be out there," Maisie called over the noise of the rain. "Are you out by yourselves? Isn't that dangerous?"

Sofia and Max exchanged a glance. "Er . . . ," Max said. "It's kind of a long story."

Sofia hurriedly changed the subject by saying, "There's another boat out there. It's yellow. And it's getting thrown about by the waves. We're really worried about the people on board!"

Maisie sighed and shook her head. "No one was on board," she said. "That's my family's boat. It broke loose during the storm."

Max blew out a breath of relief, but then noticed that Maisie looked upset.

"It's all my fault," she said. "I'm the one who tied up the boat. It's named *Bonnie* for my granny—she passed away when I was nine, but she spent her whole life sailing and taught me how. Ma will be so upset when she gets back from town and finds out!"

"I'm sorry," said Sofia. "Maybe we can help you look for it—I mean, after the

storm passes." She shivered as water seeped through her socks and shoes.

Maisie grabbed her hand. "Maybe. But let's get you inside now."

As she led them toward the red-roofed shop, Sofia took in the other waterfront buildings: a small fishing museum, a restaurant advertising fish and chips, and a large white building labeled *Animal Rescue.* She stopped walking and pointed. "Oh! Do they see a lot of sick animals in there?"

Maisie turned. "Yes. The rescue center takes in injured birds and wildlife," she said.

"But you'll see plenty of wildlife in Granddad's shop. Come on!" Her eyes twinkled as she led Max and Sofia into the shop.

Sofia sucked in her breath as she entered. The shop was filled floor to ceiling with wooden carvings of birds and animals. A seabird took flight on a shelf overhead. A giant bear loomed from a corner. And beside it, a baby bear carved of pale white pine stared sweetly at Sofia. "Aw," she murmured, stroking its smooth nose.

"Yikes, more like," said Max, nervously eyeing the bear's huge mother. He slid onto a polished oak bench and ran his fingers across the tiny leaves carved into its surface. "These are amazing!" he said. "Who makes them?"

Maisie flushed with pride. "My granddad. He's working now." Cheerful whistling trailed out of the back room, down the hall, and into the shop, making Sofia and Max grin. But Maisie's face fell. "He'll be so upset that *Bonnie* has gone. And it's all my fault."

Max and Sofia felt bad for Maisie. She obviously hadn't done it on purpose. Then Sofia spotted a sliver of sunshine behind the curtain of clouds. "The storm is passing!" she said. "We can look for *Bonnie* now."

Maisie's face brightened. "Let me ask Granddad," she said. "Do you need to ring your parents or anything?"

Max and Sofia looked at each other. "Thanks, but it will be okay."

Maisie shrugged and ran to the back of the shop.

As Sofia met Max's eyes, she crossed her fingers. She really hoped they'd be able to find *Bonnie*!

Chapter 4
A Deadly Leak

Max, Sofia, and Maisie climbed on board *Wind Rider.* Max walked over to the helm while Sofia and Maisie raised the sails. As soon as they were in the air, the boat veered left and out of the harbor, back toward where they had last seen *Bonnie.*

"Whoa," said Maisie, her eyes wide. "Who's actually sailing this thing?"

Max and Sofia shared a glance.

"Erm," said Sofia. "The truth is . . ."

"It sails itself," said Max.

Maisie looked puzzled.

"It's a smart boat!" Max added, with a chuckle Sofia understood.

Maisie frowned but let it go.

Max stood near the helm while Maisie and Sofia headed to the bow, scanning the sea for the tiny yellow boat. It was far more pleasant to be sailing without the driving wind and rain, even though it was still very cold.

"Look at all those black-and-white birds!" Max called, pointing overhead.

Maisie shaded her eyes. "Guillemots," she said with a smile. "See their bright red feet?"

Max nodded. As another black bird with white wings swooped past, it cooed a hello. Then it rejoined two others soaring toward the rocky cliffs along the shore.

"What are those birds with yellowish heads?" asked Sofia. "They're so big!" She pointed at a bird with black-tipped wings and a long bill circling the boat.

Maisie followed her gaze. "That's a gannet," she said. "The largest seabirds here in the North Sea. With a bit of luck, you'll see—"

Before she could finish, the bird dove, tucked its wings, and sailed straight toward the water. Moments later, it popped out and took flight again.

Max sucked in his breath. "We'll see what now?"

"You'll see a gannet dive for fish," said Maisie, chuckling.

"Granddad says they reach nearly a hundred kilometers per hour!"

Sofia's eyes were glued to the shoreline, where a cluster of black-and-white birds with bright orange beaks waddled across the rocks. "Are those what I think they are?" she asked.

"Puffins," said Maisie, her eyes sparkling.

Sofia was so pleased she'd been right. She'd heard about puffins in stories of her grandparents' vacation, and the birds were one of the reasons she'd wanted to see Scotland.

"They visit us only during summer. We call them clowns of the sea. They're so silly! See how they play and squabble?"

As one waddled after another, joining the clown parade, Sofia laughed. "They're so cute!"

"There's more," said Maisie. "Look." She pointed toward the water.

Sofia gasped as a dolphin leaped out of the sea. Others playfully nudged one another as they raced through the waves. "There are so many!" She started counting the fins but lost track at nine.

"Are they bottlenose dolphins?" asked Max, who had seen the gray dolphins with short snouts near Starry Bay. "I didn't know there were any in Scotland!"

Maisie's cheeks turned pink with pride. "The only dolphins in the North Sea live in Scotland. Tourists flock here to Seal Bay to see the wildlife. We're very lucky.

The *selkies*, the seals, are my favorite. Sometimes they swim alongside people who are swimming or kayaking."

"We saw the seals. And a seal pup!" said Sofia. Then her worries rushed back like water into a leaky boat. "I hope it survived the storm."

Maisie squeezed Sofia's shoulder. "The pup will be all right. Its ma will look after it. But *Bonnie* might have been done in by the storm. My ma and dad will be devastated if that wee boat is lost. . . ." She bit her lip.

"We'll find it," Sofia promised.

Moments later, as *Wind Rider* slid up alongside the rocks of Seal Bay, Maisie let out a small cry.

A tiny yellow boat, no longer than two seals stretched out end to end, lay cockeyed across the rocks. Even from the deck of *Wind Rider,* Max could see the gaping hole in the side of the little boat. "Maybe we can fix it," he said quickly. "My grandpa fixes boats—I've helped him!"

"I'm not so sure," Maisie said sadly.

As Sofia leaned over to give Maisie a hug, she spotted something. A shimmering swirl of greasy color stretched across the water between *Bonnie* and *Wind Rider*.

"*Bonnie* is leaking oil!" Sofia cried in alarm. "I did a school project on oil spills. Oil can poison sea animals—or get in their fur or wings. They can get waterlogged and drown!" As she pictured the baby seal, her stomach tensed.

Maisie pulled a phone from her pocket. "I'll call 999 for the coast guard." She dialed the number and stepped away from the rail.

Sofia paced the deck. "They won't get here soon enough. Look how the oil is spreading!" The dark, metallic liquid cast a thick sheen over the waves. "What can we do?"

Max stared at *Bonnie*. "Maybe we can soak it up somehow?" he said, thinking out loud.

As *Wind Rider* glided closer to the wrecked boat, Sofia nodded. "Yes!" she exclaimed. Then she leaned in to whisper to Max. "This must be why *Wind Rider* brought us here. We have to clean up the spill!"

Chapter 5
BIG FLOATING SAUSAGES

After *Wind Rider* dropped anchor a safe distance away from *Bonnie*, Max carefully climbed down to the rocks. The chemical smell of oil filled the air, making his nose wrinkle.

"Wait!" cried Maisie. She hurried after

him while Sofia tossed them a rope from above.

The rocks felt slippery beneath Max's feet—from the water or oil? He wasn't sure. But Maisie scrambled over them like a seal pup eager to get back to her mother. When she reached *Bonnie*, she knelt down beside the cracked hull.

As Max tied the rope to secure *Bonnie* to *Wind Rider*, he watched the oil drip, drip, drip from the hull. "Is it slowing down at all?" he asked.

"I think so," said Maisie. "That's good,

but . . ." She stared sadly at the pool of oil that had already spread.

"So how do we soak it up?" asked Max.

Sofia squeezed her eyes shut, trying to remember the report she had written for school. Suddenly she had it. "Big floating sausages!" she shouted over the rail.

"Huh?" said Max. "Are you feeling okay, Sofia?"

"Not *real* sausages," said Sofia with a laugh. "They're called *booms*,

66

but they look like big sausages. They're used to stop the oil from spreading, along with big pads that soak it up. Do we have anything like that?"

Maisie lifted a seat at the back of *Bonnie*, which hid a storage compartment. She pulled out a life preserver and some rope, and then sat back on her heels. "We don't," she said with a sigh.

"But wait . . . we do!" said Max. "We have some *really* absorbent blankets belowdecks on *Wind Rider*. Remember the hot chocolate I spilled, Sofia?"

Sofia's eyes lit up. "Yes! Max, you're a genius. Come help me!"

As Max and Maisie climbed back onto the sailboat, Sofia raced across the deck. She threw open the hatch and slid down the metal ladder. One blanket was still spread out on the table, a big chocolate stain in the center. She grabbed that, along with more blankets and cushions from the trunk, just as Max led Maisie down the ladder.

"Load me up," said Max. He took some blankets from Sofia.

"Me too!" said Maisie.

Sofia handed her a pile of cushions. As she pulled the last blanket out of the trunk, she saw something else. "Perfect!" She gathered up the pool noodles.

"So *that's* what we're supposed to do with them!" Max exclaimed, shaking his head. "*Wind Rider* always gives us exactly what we need."

Sofia bit her lip and nodded. "Let's hope they work."

Once they were all back on the rocks by *Bonnie*, Sofia showed them how to wrap the pool noodles in blankets and set them

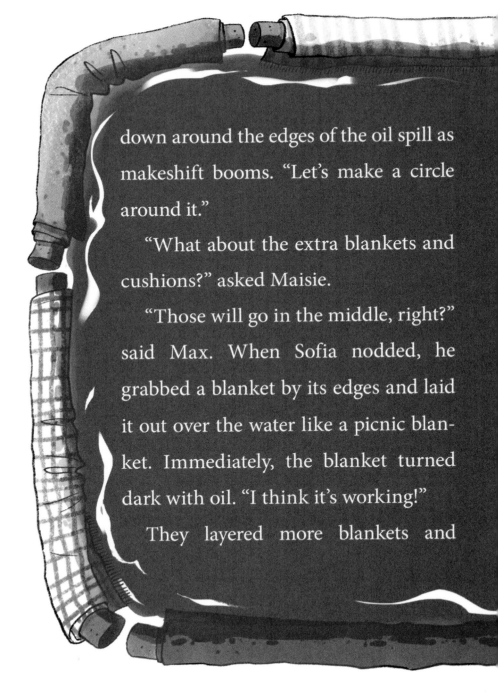

down around the edges of the oil spill as makeshift booms. "Let's make a circle around it."

"What about the extra blankets and cushions?" asked Maisie.

"Those will go in the middle, right?" said Max. When Sofia nodded, he grabbed a blanket by its edges and laid it out over the water like a picnic blanket. Immediately, the blanket turned dark with oil. "I think it's working!"

They layered more blankets and

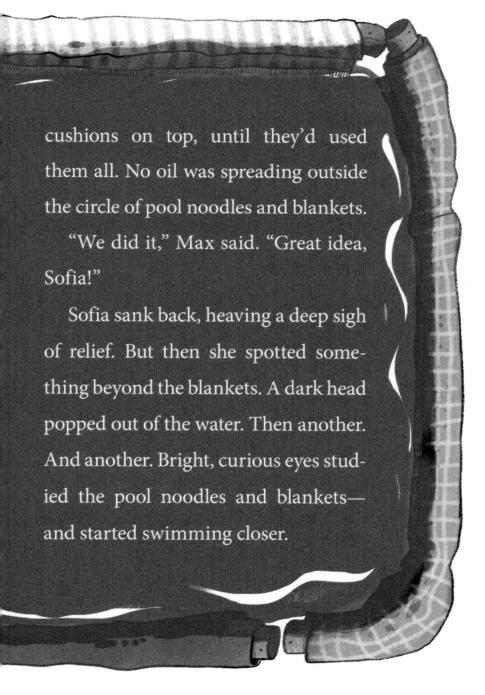

cushions on top, until they'd used them all. No oil was spreading outside the circle of pool noodles and blankets.

"We did it," Max said. "Great idea, Sofia!"

Sofia sank back, heaving a deep sigh of relief. But then she spotted something beyond the blankets. A dark head popped out of the water. Then another. And another. Bright, curious eyes studied the pool noodles and blankets—and started swimming closer.

"The seals!" Sofia cried. Her throat was tight. "They're swimming straight toward the oil spill. We have to stop them!"

Chapter 6
A PUP IN PERiL

Sofia waved her arms and jumped up and down, trying to scare the seals into swimming the other way. But they only swam closer, as if they were curious about the silly girl dancing on their rocks.

"Wait, I've got an idea!" Max quickly

climbed back on board *Wind Rider* and slid belowdecks. He reappeared a moment later, holding the kite.

"It distracted the seals before," he called over the railing. "Let's see if it works again!" He ran toward the stern of the boat and pulled at the string of the kite, making it swoop up and down, like it was dancing in the wind, high above the seal herd. "Hey, seals!" he called. "Check this out!"

Sofia held her breath and watched. One by one, the seals stopped. They turned

their sleek heads away from the oil spill, toward the bobbing kite. And they began to swim. "Yes!" she cheered. "Keep going!"

But *Wind Rider* was still tied to *Bonnie*, so they weren't far enough from the spill. "We have to set sail," Max called. "We have to get farther away. Untie the rope. Hurry!"

Maisie glanced sadly at the rope that connected *Bonnie* to *Wind Rider.*

"We'll come back for your boat," Sofia said softly. "I promise."

Maisie set her jaw and nodded. Then she quickly untied the rope.

When the girls were back on *Wind Rider*, the boat seemed to know what to do. Slowly, it raised its anchor and drifted away from the oil spill. Max tied the kite to the rail so that it flew above the seals.

"They're all following us," said Sofia, breathing a sigh of relief. "Wait, all except one." One small, dark head turned away

from the others and headed back *toward* the rocks. "It's the baby!" she realized with horror. "Where is it going?"

Her eyes tracked the path of the pup, straight back to the rocks. There, beside the wrecked *Bonnie*, a large seal struggled to climb out of the water. Even from afar, Sofia could see dark oil streaked across the seal's back. Her stomach dropped.

"The pup is swimming back to its ma!" Maisie cried.

"And she's got oil on her!" Sofia shouted. "Quick! We have to stop the pup from going in the oil, too!" She put a foot on the rail, as if she were about to jump overboard.

Max grabbed Sofia's hand. "You can't swim to them," he said. "You'll freeze!"

Sofia's eyes widened. "We have wet suits," she remembered. "And the kayak—seals like kayaks. Maisie said so!"

Maisie bobbed her head in agreement. "Yes," she said. "The *selkie* might follow the kayak!"

At those words, Sofia took off running toward the hatch, with Max close behind. By the time they had pulled on their wet suits, Maisie had inflated the orange kayak using a battery-powered pump. Then she helped them lower it overboard.

"Let me sit in back," said Max. "I'll steer, and you can sit up front and talk to the seal pup."

"Be careful and don't get too close," Maisie warned. "The seals are wild, and that pup's ma won't like you going near her baby."

Max and Sofia began paddling. But the waves were so strong! Max struggled with each stroke. He switched sides, paddling first on the left and then on the right, trying to keep the kayak on course. "Do you see the pup?" he called to Sofia.

She took another stroke and searched the waves. The seal pup's dark head popped

out of the water. "There!" she cried, pointing at the spot, a few yards away.

As the pup swiveled its head to look at them, the mother barked a warning from the rocks. It responded with a cry of its own. *"Mah, mah!"* The sound nearly broke Sofia's heart.

"What now?" Max whispered.

Sofia splashed the water playfully with her paddle until the pup turned again.

Then she twirled the end of the paddle, creating a kaleidoscope of orange. The seal swam closer, then closer still, until Sofia could see its sweet face and shiny black eyes.

"It's working!" Max whispered. "Sofia, you're a seal whisperer!"

Sofia could barely breathe as the pup swam a full circle around the kayak. As it passed, it lifted its muzzle and sniffed at them, as if to say hello.

Sofia's heart leaped. "Hello, my sweet *selkie*," she cooed, using Maisie's word for *seal*.

"Hello, little one," Max whispered from

behind. Then something caught his eye. Maisie was waving from *Wind Rider* and pointing back toward the cliffs where the puffins nested. "She's showing us where the other seals went," said Max. "Can you make the pup follow us, Sofia?"

Sofia met Max's eyes, swallowed hard, and then nodded. She had to try!

As Max set his course and began paddling, Sofia kept watch to make sure the seal pup was following. Whenever it seemed distracted, she twirled her paddle and called gently to it. Slowly, stroke by stroke, they crossed the choppy sea, with the seal pup close behind.

When they finally reached the rocks where the other seals were sunning, Max slowed the kayak to a crawl.

"Time to join your family," he called to the seal pup. "Go on now."

The pup waited near the kayak, as if wondering whether Max and Sofia were coming, too.

"It's all right," Sofia said. "We'll wait for you right here." She crossed her fingers, hoping the pup would know what to do.

At last, it dove underwater and reappeared near the cluster of rocks. When it pulled itself onto a rock and snuggled next to a large spotted seal, Sofia finally let out her breath.

A motor sounded from the harbor, startling Max. He turned and saw several red boats with yellow stripes zooming toward them on the waves.

"It's the coast guard!" he cried.

"Hooray!" Sofia cheered.

She only hoped they would be in time to save the mama seal.

CHAPTER 7
A SPLASHY REUNION

Sofia kicked nervously at the leg of her chair as they sat in the reception area of the animal rescue center, a room lined with framed photos of seabirds and animals.

It had been only a couple of hours since the coast guard had brought the mama seal here to clean the oil off her fur. But for Sofia, it felt more like days. She leaned her head against Maisie's shoulder and wondered if the mama had been reunited with her pup yet. The rescue team had brought the pup in, too, because it was too young to survive without its mother.

"We'll hear something soon," said Max. "Don't worry."

Maisie suddenly sat up straight in her chair. "Ma! Dad!" she said, looking over at the doorway. "You're here!"

A ginger-haired woman stepped into

the waiting area, a worried expression on her face, followed by a man in a cap who was pale with fright. When the woman spread her arms, Maisie leaped out of her chair and ran to her mother. "I'm sorry," Maisie cried. "I'm so sorry about *Bonnie*!"

"Hush now," said her mother. "The winds were strong and no one was hurt. *Bonnie* has had a good long life."

As Maisie wiped a tear away, Max swallowed the lump in his throat. He knew Maisie was thinking about her granny.

"There'll be a new *Bonnie*," Maisie's dad soothed her.

Max's ears perked right up. "You know how to build a boat?"

Maisie's dad grinned. "We do. With a little help from Granddad. And it's *possible* we've nearly finished it already." He winked at Maisie.

"Wait, you have?" Maisie's eyes widened. "Really?"

Her dad ruffled up her hair. "Yes, sweet girl, we have." He turned back toward Max. "We've known for a while now that the original *Bonnie* would have to be retired. Running an engine like that isn't environmentally friendly, as the oil spill shows. The new *Bonnie* is an eco-sailboat made from recycled wood. It uses only wind for power, so there will be no oil to leak."

"That's so cool!" said Max.

The door to the waiting area opened and

a rescue worker stepped through. She wore rubber gloves and a white, water-spattered apron with a name tag that said *Lucy*. "I heard there were some visitors here who might like to see their seal friends," Lucy said with a bright smile.

"Yes!" Sofia was first through the door. She followed Lucy down the long, winding hall.

In a room at the end, two seals were splashing around in a big blue plastic tub. Sofia recognized the big-eyed baby right away, and the large spotted seal beside it

had to be its mother—she kept nosing at it, as if to make sure it was okay. And the pup nipped at her flippers, as if to say, *Where have you been?*

As Max and Maisie stepped into the room behind her, Sofia turned to face Lucy. "Is the mother seal all right? Will she be okay?"

Lucy nodded. "You were right to call the coast guard when you did. Although she had lots of oil on her fur, she doesn't seem to have swallowed any."

Max stepped closer to the tub. "But how did you clean her up so quickly? She was completely covered!" He shuddered at the memory.

"Seal fur is usually thin and easy to clean," Lucy explained. "And fortunately, the rest of the seals were spotted far away from the spill, so they're okay, too. You all did a very good thing today. You saved this mother seal and her wee boy. We're going to release them into a safe, quiet cove tomorrow morning—at West Beach beside the village. Would you like to join us?"

"Yes!" exclaimed Maisie. She looked toward Max and Sofia. "Will you come, too?"

Max and Sofia smiled at each other.

"Maybe we could have a sleepover on *Wind Rider*?" Sofia whispered. Just the thought of staying an extra day sent a jolt of excitement from her head to her toes.

"Yes!" Max's eyes lit up. "We might need *Wind Rider* to give us a few new blankets, though."

"What do you say?" Maisie asked. She reached for their hands and squeezed.

"We'll be there." Sofia squeezed back and grinned.

CHAPTER 8
INTO THE WAVES

"There are so many!" said Sofia, leaning over the rail of *Wind Rider.* She shaded her eyes, marveling at all the seals sunbathing on West Beach. And soon, there would be two more.

Max and Sofia had dropped anchor in

the bay for the night, but now *Wind Rider* was carrying them toward the beach. As it slid alongside the dock, Max took a deep breath. "Sofia, it's the new *Bonnie!*"

He pointed at the sleek new sailboat bobbing beside the dock. Its hull, made of chestnut-brown reclaimed wood, gleamed in the morning light. And *Bonnie* was painted in cheery yellow letters across the polished boards.

"It's beautiful!" Sofia cried. Then she spotted Maisie and her parents on the beach. There was a white-haired elderly man with them, wrapped up in a thick coat, who had to be Maisie's granddad. "Let's go!"

Max quickly tied up *Wind Rider* and raced down the dock after Sofia. Across the beach, Maisie, her granddad, and her

parents stood beside Lucy and a large white truck. "It's almost time!" Maisie called to them, bouncing on her toes.

From the truck, rescue-center workers clad in blue carefully slid out two large carrying cases. "They look like the cage we use to bring our pup to the vet," Maisie said.

Max laughed. "That one is carrying a different kind of pup," he said, pointing. The seal pup peered out the wire door at the end of the cage. He pawed at it with his flipper and let out a pitiful cry. *"Mah, mah!"*

His mother grunted in response from the cage next to him as the rescue-center workers carried each cage down the beach toward the water. Lucy waved the kids over. "Come watch," she said.

"Just stand back a bit so you don't startle them."

She and another worker slowly opened the wire doors to both cages and then stepped away.

The mama seal wriggled out of her cage, slowly at first. When the seal pup saw her, he hopped through the door of his own carrier and waddled across the sand.

Sofia giggled. "He's so happy!" she whispered.

Once the mother seal reached the safety of the tide, she turned and nuzzled her pup. But they didn't dive into the waves right away. They splashed and played together in the shallows, the pup nipping at his mother and sliding on and off her back.

"What a show-off!" said Max, chuckling.

Gradually, the seals swam farther and farther away—until they were gone. "Time to say goodbye," said Sofia. She smiled sadly and gave a little wave.

When a bird cawed overhead, Max glanced up, hoping to see a gannet diving for fish. Instead, he saw a seagull—a very familiar-looking one. The bird swooped so low, Max felt his hair ruffle. He nudged Sofia. "I think it's time for us to say good-bye, too."

When she saw the seagull, Sofia met Max's gaze and sighed.

"You have to go?" said Maisie. Her shoulders drooped. "Wait, I have something for you." She dug in her pockets and pulled out two carved figures.

"Seals!" said Sofia. "Oh, they're so cute." She cupped her golden-brown seal in her palm, admiring its sweet, puppylike face.

Max ran his finger over the smooth head of his seal. "Wow—did your grand-dad make them?"

Maisie shook her head. "I did. Well, Granddad helped me a little." She flashed a smile back at her granddad, who was waiting with her parents. "They're to thank you. And so you'll always remember me and the *selkies*."

Sofia's heart swelled. "I know just where

we'll put them," she said, picturing the wooden shelf of treasures in the cabin of *Wind Rider*.

A short while later, Sofia and Max stood on the deck of their boat, waving to Maisie and her family, back on the dock. *Wind Rider* carried them out into the harbor, until even the new *Bonnie* was just a speck across the gray-blue sea.

Then the wind began to blow.

"It's time," said Max with a grin. "Hold on tight." He gripped his carved seal with one hand and the rail with the other.

Sofia braced herself beside him, squeezing her eyes shut but smiling wide. *I kayaked with a baby seal*, she told herself. *Best. Adventure. Ever!*

As the world spun around her, she pictured her twirling kayak paddle and how the baby *selkie* had watched it with sweet, curious eyes. Before she knew it, the deck below her feet stopped rocking and the wind became a gentle breeze.

"Home, sweet home!" said Max, inhaling the damp scent of the mangrove forest in Starry Bay. He let go of the rail, now weathered and worn, and began to cross the warped deck of the old sailboat. *Wind Rider* was resting once again, leaning into the earth as if they'd never been gone at all.

"Wait! Let's put these belowdecks," said Sofia, holding up her seal.

Max followed her down the ladder into the cabin. As Sofia placed the carved seals next to their other treasures, Max reached

for something else—the red box kite that had led the seals away from danger. "Do you have time for a little more kite flying today?"

Sofia nodded eagerly. "There's *always* time for one more adventure," she said with a wink. Then she and Max scampered up the metal ladder and out into the sunshine.

THE *WIND RIDER* LOGBOOK

Sofia's sketch of *Wind Rider*

caBin

hElm

STeRn

hull

mast

SeaGull

Sail

porThole

bow

windRIDER

anchoR

OUR SCOTTISH ADVENTURE

Wind Rider brought us to Scotland, which is the northernmost part of the United Kingdom. (The other parts are England, Wales, and Northern Ireland.) Scotland is surrounded by the Atlantic Ocean, and off its east coast is the North Sea. Many interesting animals live in Scotland and around its coasts, such as seals, gannets, stoats, puffins, and even dolphins! Unfortunately, many of these creatures are endangered and face problems like habitat destruction and lack of food.

Orkney
Islands

Atlantic Ocean

North Sea

er
des

HIGHLANDS

SCOTLAND

LOWLANDS

Northern
Ireland

Irish Sea

England

MAX'S HARBOR SEAL FACTS

We loved playing with harbor seals in Scotland! Here are my top harbor seal facts.

- All harbor seals have a fatty layer under their skin called blubber. This keeps them warm when they are swimming in cold water. Blubber also stores nutrients as an emergency energy source and helps seals easily stay afloat. Swimming is tiring and takes up a lot of energy!

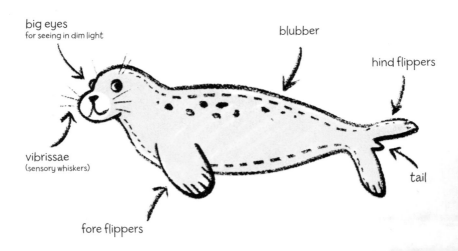

big eyes
for seeing in dim light

blubber

hind flippers

vibrissae
(sensory whiskers)

tail

fore flippers

▮ Harbor seals are amazing divers. They can swim down as far as one thousand six hundred feet (that's more than the height of the Empire State Building) and hold their breath for up to twenty-eight minutes!

▮ When seals sunbathe on a beach in large numbers, it's called a haul-out. They usually do this to rest or to find a mate.

▮ One of the biggest dangers baby seals face is getting caught in fishing nets by mistake.

SOFIA'S OIL SPILL FACTS

Oil spills can happen when boats carrying oil are wrecked or when oil wells that are pumping oil from beneath the seabed get damaged.

An oil spill is very bad for sea life. Birds, seals, and sea otters that get covered in oil can't clean themselves. They have to be caught and then cleaned by humans with a special detergent. The thinner fur on seals means they are easier to clean than birds with many feathers or furry animals like otters. It can take up to three hundred gallons of water to get one bird clean.

It's very hard to clean up oil spills, but here are some of the best methods:

Booms—these are floating barriers that can be put around the edge of an oil slick to stop it spreading any farther.

Sorbents—these are very absorbent materials that are dipped in the water to soak up oil.

Skimmers—these are like special vacuum cleaners that suck the oil up from the surface of the water. The oil can then be recycled and used as an ingredient for other materials such as rubber.

HOW CAN WE HELP PREVENT OIL SPILLS?

We can prevent oil spills by reducing our need for oil and using renewable energy instead— that's energy that comes from naturally replenishing sources like the wind, the sun, moving water, or even from heat deep beneath the earth. Does your home get energy from solar panels or wind turbines?

Wind from the west. fish bite the best.
Wind from the east. fish bite the least.
Wind from the north. do not go forth.
Wind from the south blows bait in their mouth.

This is an old proverb . . . and like many old proverbs, there is some truth in it! However, it's not the wind that makes the fishing conditions better, but the changes in temperature and weather that usually go with the change in wind direction.